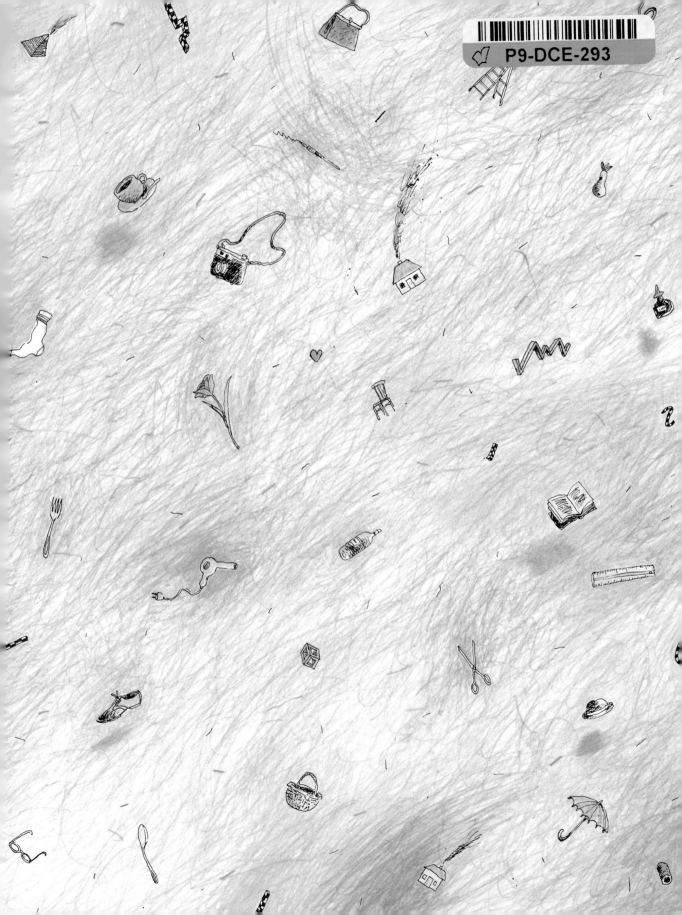

HENRIK DRESCHER

LOTHROP, LEE & SHEPARD BOOKS · NEW YORK

The Strange Appearance of Howard Cranebill, Jr.

Library of Congress Cataloging in Publication Data
Drescher, Henrik.   The strange appearance of Howard Cranebill, Jr.
Summary: Having long wished for a child, Mr. and Mrs. Cranebill are delighted with the baby
they discover on their doorstep even though he has an unusually long and pointy nose.
[1. Storks—Fiction.   2. Babies—Fiction]   I. Title.
PZ7.D78383St   [E]   82-71
ISBN 0-688-00961-1   AACR2
ISBN 0-688-00962-X (lib. bdg.)

For
Theresa

With Special Thanks To
Barbara Lalicki, Steven Heller
and
Julie Quan.

Mr. and Mrs. Cranebill lived all alone in a little house with a pear tree in the backyard.

Their biggest wish was to have a child, and one morning when they opened their door they found a basket at their feet, with a little baby lying in it, all wrapped up.

The Dog

When they unwrapped the child they saw that it had sparkly eyes, a plump little belly, and an unusually long and pointy nose.

The baby was taken to the most accomplished overgrown-nose doctors, who felt, measured, looked, and poked at him for many hours.

They were distressed to admit that they had never seen a nose *that* long and pointy before. Further, they knew no cure for it.

So Mr. and Mrs. Cranebill ignored the
nose, named the baby Howard, Jr., and
proceeded to hug and cuddle him as
parents are supposed to do.

When Howard started to crawl
he had to be helped out of some pretty
nosey situations, like being stuck
in the wall, or…

...getting tangled up at
the zoo.

old
Elephant

He had a lot
of trouble with
doughnuts,

and he always seemed to be dipping
his nose into the wrong things.

Howard liked to
climb and hide.

One day, when no one was looking,
Howard crawled into the backyard and
started climbing the big pear tree.

He had to be helped down.

A few days later Howard climbed even
farther, and a ladder was needed to get
him down.

During supper Howard's mind was on the pear tree.

That night, after
Mr. and Mrs. Cranebill
were asleep, Howard
crept out his window
and headed for the
garden.

The next morning Mr. and Mrs. Cranebill were awakened by high-pitched singing in the garden. They went out, sleepy-eyed, to investigate.

There at the top of the pear tree sat little Howard, singing to a beautiful stork.

Even with their tallest ladder, the fire department couldn't reach him.

Mr. and Mrs. Cranebill called and cried to Howard, but he was too comfortable to come back down.

Howard stayed in the pear tree for
many days and nights.

One morning Mrs. Cranebill looked up
and saw that Howard had changed.

His arms had become feathery wings and his chubby little legs had changed into long, graceful stork legs.

The unusually long and pointy nose didn't seem out of place any more.

AT DUSK ... they FLEW

That afternoon, every stork gathered to sing a
farewell song to Mr. and Mrs. Cranebill. At dusk
they left in small groups, flying south for the
winter as storks do each year.

The last to leave the pear tree was Howard.
He flapped his newly formed wings through the
night air and soon joined the other birds on their
long journey.

Mr. and Mrs. Cranebill were sad to say good-bye to their son Howard, but they knew he would return the following spring, to build his nest in the tall pear tree in the backyard.

The End

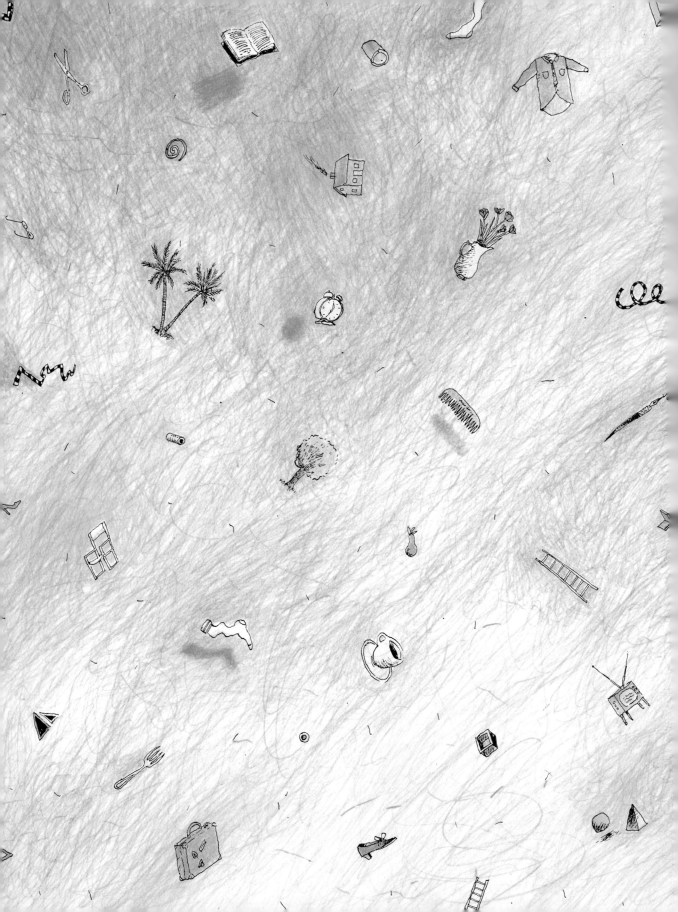